RUMBLE
TUMBLE

BEN NEWMAN

The bear goes…

...BUMP!

...FLUMP!

The bees go
BUZZ, BUZZ!

The snake goes
HISS, HISS!

The tortoise goes GRUNT, GRUNT!

The raccoon and the wolf go...

...EEK, EEK,

Everyone goes
RUMBLE...

...TUMBLE...

HOWL, HOWL!

...OOF!

The bees, the snake,
the tortoise, the raccoon
and the wolf, all go
WAH, WAH!

The bear goes…

. . . AHA!

The sandwich is YUM, YUM!

Everyone goes BYE-BYE!

Inspired by and dedicated to Ernie Newman,
our clumsy little daredevil – B.N.

First published 2021 by Macmillan Children's Books
an imprint of Pan Macmillan
The Smithson,
6 Briset Street,
London EC1M 5NR
EU representative: Macmillan Publishers Ireland Limited,
Mallard Lodge, Lansdowne Village, Dublin 4

Associated companies throughout the world

www.panmacmillan.com

ISBN: 978-1-5290-5146-9

135798642

A CIP catalogue record for this book is available from
the British Library.

Printed in China

FSC
www.fsc.org

MIX
Paper from
responsible sources
FSC® C116313